BLO/Cn

The Fairground Ghost

Felicity Everett
Adapted by Lesley Sims

Illustrated by Alex de Wolf

Reading Consultant: Alison Kelly
Roehampton University

Contents

Chapter 1

All the fun of the fair

On Friday, Jake Hubbard saw
a poster on his way to school.
The fair was in town.

That night, Jake was so excited, he could hardly sleep. The next day was Saturday. At last, he could go to the fair.

But first, he had to find someone to go with him.

I think I'll ask Dad.

4

Dad wasn't even dressed.
How could he be busy?

Dad shook his paper at Jake.
Jake tried his mother.

Will you take me to
the fair? Please?

"There are 70 great attractions!"
Jake told her.

"And I've got 70 great piles
of washing to iron," she said.
"Why not ask your sister?"

7

Jake made a face. His sister Marcia spent the whole time on the phone. But he had to find someone to go with. He went to ask Marcia.

Brad was Marcia's boyfriend.
Jake groaned. She could be on the
phone for hours.

"But it's open now," Jake said.
Marcia glared at him.
"It shuts at ten!" Jake added.
"Shhh!" said Marcia.

Shh! I can't
hear Brad!

Jake held his breath. He counted to ten. He counted to ten again. At last, Marcia looked up.

"OK, pest," she said. "We'll take you."

Hooray!

Jake ran to his piggy bank and shook out the coins. He was going to the fair!

Chapter 2

Ghost train

Jake, Marcia
and Brad
walked
into the
fairground.

Lights flashed. People laughed. Twenty different pop songs blared out at once.

Look over there!

Marcia and Brad headed
straight for the Tunnel of Love.
"Yuck!" said Jake. "That's silly."
Jake wanted something scary.

In fact,
Jake wanted
something
really scary.

Jake found a sign which pointed to five attractions. He knew the ride for him! The ghost train. It sounded perfect.

He soon found
the ghost train and
climbed aboard.

With a lurch, the train
began to move into a tunnel.

16

Suddenly, the train was in darkness. Glowing ghouls and scary skeletons jumped out of the blackness.

People shrieked. The ghosts moaned back.

Jake was delighted. He'd wanted a scary ride and this was very, very scary.

He was so busy watching a vampire leap from its coffin...

...he didn't see what was lurking behind him. Jake screamed.

He was so scared his goose
bumps had goose bumps.

Then the train went around
the final bend and out popped
a little ghost.

WHOOOOO

But the little ghost wasn't scary.
The little ghost was the funniest
thing Jake had ever seen.

Chapter 3

The scare-o-meter

Jake was still laughing as he left the train.

"What's so funny?" asked a man with a clipboard.

What could make you laugh on a ghost train?

"The little ghost!" gasped Jake.
He hadn't seen the man's badge.
He didn't know the man was a
Ghost Inspector.

The man sounded cross. Jake
was worried.

The Ghost Inspector went to
see the owner of the ghost train.

"Did you know you have
a *funny* ghost on your ghost
train?" he said. "I want to see
that ghost now!"

The owner of the ghost train was surprised. But he couldn't argue with the Ghost Inspector. So he called for the little ghost.

Jake began to wish he hadn't laughed. The Ghost Inspector was looking very angry indeed.

"Wait till I test that ghost on my scare-o-meter!" he said.

The little ghost appeared. It didn't look so funny now.

"Out you go!" said the owner of the ghost train. "You have to be tested."

The little ghost was terrified.

Jake could hardly bear to watch.
What would happen to the little
ghost if it failed the test?

Chapter 4

Ghost test

The Ghost Inspector held up his scare-o-meter.

"Be as scary as you can," he said to the little ghost.

The little ghost took a
deep breath...

...and screamed.

The arrow on the scare-o-meter
quivered. Was the little ghost
scary? The Inspector checked.

"Just as I thought!" he said. "Not
scary at all."

"Get out!" the owner of the ghost train shouted at the little ghost. "And don't come back!"

"No funny ghosts allowed on my train," he added.

"Quite right too," said the Ghost Inspector. "Funny ghosts indeed! Whatever next?"

The little ghost started to
glide sadly away.

Jake ran after it. "Wait!" he
shouted. "Hey! Don't go."

He tried to catch hold of the
little ghost.

"Don't be sad!" Jake said,
when he caught up with the ghost.
"This is a fun fair. Why not stay
and have some fun?"

Come on!
What shall we
do first?

Chapter 5

Fair scare

Jake decided to take the ghost for a ride. No one could be sad on a merry-go-round.

Jake was right. The little ghost wasn't sad. It was scared to death.

32

Jake decided to try the roller
coaster instead. The little ghost
wasn't sure.

"Well..." it said.

Jake dragged it along.

Roller Coaster

"It's so exciting. Just wait
till you get on. You'll love it!"
Jake said.

Jake was right. At first, the little ghost did love it.

"This is fun!" it said, as it sat down. Then the ride started...

Jake was thrilled. They curved around corners and looped the loop. He whooped with delight. The little ghost did not whoop. It turned green.

Jake waved to everyone in the fairground below. The little ghost couldn't look. For the rest of the ride, it kept its eyes shut tight.

The little ghost left the roller
coaster a very sorry spook.

Jake thought hard. He had
to cheer up his new friend. But
how? Just then, he had an idea.

I've got it!
Follow me!

Chapter 6

A huge scary ghost

Jake was so excited, he started to run. The little ghost pulled back.

"Where are we going?" it asked. "Promise it's not scary."

"I promise!" said Jake. "Now, close your eyes!" he added.

"Are you sure it's not scary?" asked the shivering spook.

"No scarier than you are," said Jake.

The little ghost wasn't convinced.

"Where are we?" the little ghost whimpered.

"Nearly there," said Jake. "You can open your eyes..."

"...now!"

"AAAAGGGGHHHH!" screamed the little ghost, as it caught sight of its own reflection.

It rushed out of the tent, wailing at the top of its voice.

"AAAAGGGGHHHH!"

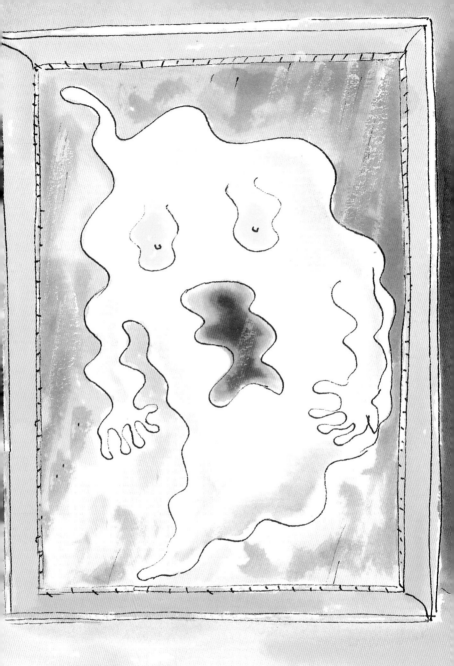

45

WHAAAA!

Shooting Gallery

The eerie howls
of the little ghost
echoed around
the fairground.
Nearly everyone
was terrified.

47

Jake ran after the little ghost. "Come back!" he cried.

"I can't!" said the little ghost. "That huge scary ghost will catch me."

That huge scary ghost was you!

The little ghost stopped
suddenly. Was Jake right?
"That scary ghost was me?
Really? Are you sure? Me?"
it babbled.

Jake and the little ghost went to find the owner of the ghost train. Perhaps he would give the little ghost another chance.

Won't you take it back, now you've heard how scary it is?

But the owner of the ghost train hadn't even noticed the little ghost terrify the fairground.

What did you say? I can't hear a word.

Jake pleaded with the man
to test the ghost again with the
scare-o-meter.

The man agreed although he
thought it would be a waste of time.

OK, but it
doesn't seem any
different to me.

Everyone watched as Jake
held up the scare-o-meter.
   The little ghost took a deep
breath, lifted its arms
and screamed.

NOT A BIT
SCARY

A LITTLE
SCARY

SCARY

VERY
SCARY

TERRIFYING

HELP!

SCARE-O-METER

It was a blood-
curdling scream.
Even Dracula
was scared.

AAAAH!

The Ghost Inspector had
to admit that the little ghost
was terrifying.

The owner of the ghost train
was delighted. "Look at that!"
he said to the Ghost Inspector.

"Welcome back!" he said to the ghost. "You'll be the new star of the show."

Everyone was delighted to have the little ghost back. Well, almost everyone.

With the little ghost back and scarier than it had ever been, the ghost train became the busiest ride in the fairground.

People stood for hours, just to see the little ghost.

Some people were so scared,
they came out looking like the
zombies inside.

Then they staggered around the fairground with their knees knocking... before going back for another turn.

The little ghost had never
been happier – or scarier.

As for Jake, he got every ride
free, thanks to his friend, the
fairground ghost.

Try these other books in
Series Two:

The Incredible Present: Lily gets everything she's ever wished for... but things don't turn out as she expects.

The Clumsy Crocodile: Cassy, the clumsiest crocodile in town, is about to start her new job – as a shop assistant in a china department...

Designed by
Katarina Dragoslović
and Maria Wheatley

This edition first published in 2007 by Usborne Publishing Ltd.,
Usborne House, 83-85 Saffron Hill, London EC1N 8RT, England.
www.usborne.com
Copyright © 2007, 2002, 1996, 1995 Usborne Publishing Ltd.